Adventures of a Texas Blue Heeler

GUNNER MEETS DAISY

Amy Jo Wallace

Illustrated by
Stephanie Fliss Dumas

adventurestexasblue.com

Adventures of a Texas Blue Heeler: Gunner Meets Daisy

For more information, please contact:
Texas Blue Publishing
2701 Pecan Meadow Drive
Garland, TX 75040
adventuresoftexasblue@gmail.com

Library of Congress Control Number: 2021920851

ISBN 978-1-7361114-2-0

Printed in the United States

Dedicated to...

Inez Wallace

Buttercup is safe and happy in her forever home; thanks to a wonderful animal rescue organization. I know you are smiling and watching over us from the pink skies above.

Howdy! My name is Gunner. I'm a handsome blue heeler from Texas and **ONE LUCKY DOG**.

My life is good. I have an awesome backyard,
pretty decent meals and a family who loves me.

I have a hankering for tennis balls
and my week is full of them…

On **Monday**, I guard the
backyard from pesky squirrels,

I help my family water the garden,

and I play **hold the tennis ball**.

But…when my people leave, when it's quiet,

I'm lonely and I've been known to get into mischief…

On **Tuesday**, I guard the
backyard from pesky squirrels,

I patrol the neighborhood for litter clean up,

and I play **catch the tennis ball off the roof**...
hopefully right into my mouth!

I'm lonely and I've been known to get a little ornery…

On **Wednesdays**, I guard the backyard from pesky squirrels,

I help my family push out the recycling cart for pick up,

and I play **fetch the tennis ball.**

Did I mention I have an
appreciation for tennis balls?

But…when my people leave, when it's quiet,

I'm lonely and I've been
known to get into mischief…

On **Thursday**, I guard the backyard from pesky squirrels,

I escort my family to the grocery store,

and I play **find the squeaker**...
my record time is under one minute.

But...when my people leave, when it's quiet,
I'm lonely and a little sad...

On **Friday**, I guard the backyard from pesky squirrels,

I patrol the neighborhood **park** for litter clean up,

and I rest, **WHEW**, it's been a long week!
The weekend is here and my family is home...*Yee Haw!*

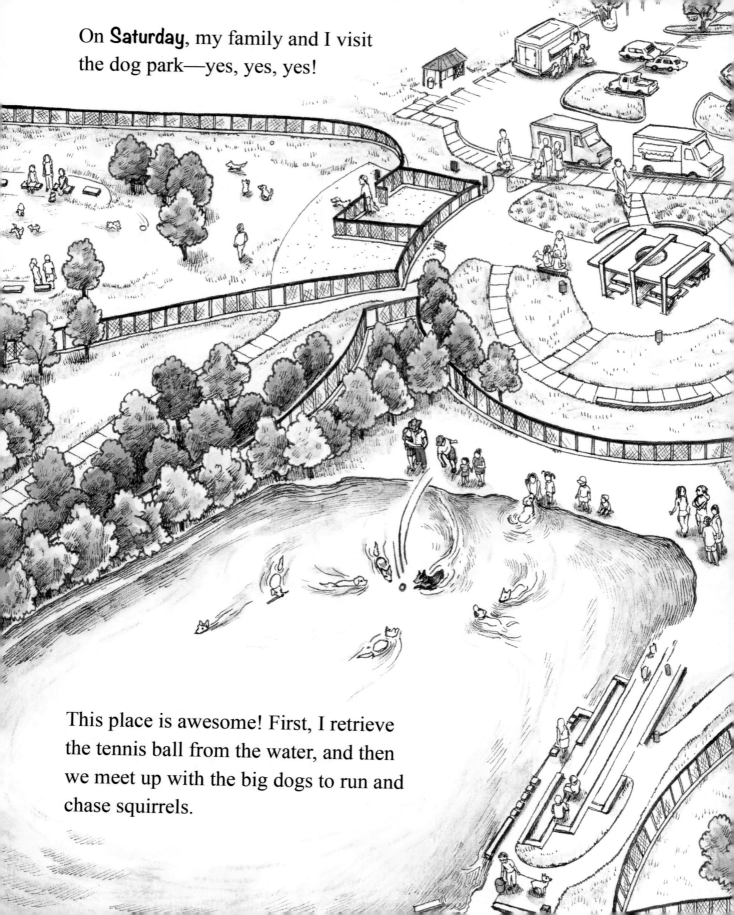

On **Saturday**, my family and I visit the dog park—yes, yes, yes!

This place is awesome! First, I retrieve the tennis ball from the water, and then we meet up with the big dogs to run and chase squirrels.

On this particular Saturday, something different happened. My family learned that a lost **blue heeler** was found and taken to a local animal shelter.

My family thinks it would be a good idea to find a friend
so I won't be lonely and perhaps I'd be a little less ornery.
Can you guess where we stopped on the way home?

Look at this place! There are all kinds of animals without homes staying here until a new home—**a forever home**—is found.

We walked through the shelter until we found the blue
heeler—**Daisy**. She was scared and did not want to look at us.
The shelter volunteers moved her into the play area where
we could check each other out... see if we liked each other.

My family adopted Daisy. It took some time but we've become good friends! We guard the backyard from the pesky squirrels together, we clean up the neighborhood together and we chase tennis balls together. I've learned to share with her, protect her and neither one of us is lonely anymore.

I look forward to the adventures Daisy
and I will have. I hope you do too!

Gunner shares a few tips about adopting a pet...

What is the difference between an animal shelter or an animal rescue organization?

Most communities have **animal shelters** that are funded by taxes that your parents/caregivers pay (ask your parent/caregiver to explain taxes to you). These shelters house all kinds of lost or surrendered animals and they take care of these animals while they try to find them a forever home—this is where you and I can make a difference!

An **animal rescue organization** is operated by a group of people who have come together to take care of lost or surrendered animals. They operate on donations and gifts, they don't have a place to house the animals, they have people who have volunteered to care for or foster animals until they can find them a forever home—this is where you and I can make a difference!

What is the best place for you to adopt or rescue a pet?

The choice is up to you! Have your parent or caretaker help you research your local area. The main difference between the two organizations is time and money. You can adopt an animal fairly quickly for a lower price at your local shelter; where as, a rescue organization takes their time to make certain the animal is a good fit for a family.

Amy Jo lives in Dallas, Texas with her husband. They share custody of the sweet pair of blue heelers, Gunner & Daisy, with their son. Amy is inspired by the beauty of wide open spaces; she loves to play tennis, ride her bike and drink tea. She is the author of the *Adventures of a Texas Blue Heeler* series.

Other books in the series:
Gunner Cleans up the Neighborhood

LOOK OUT FOR MORE
Adventures of a Texas Blue Heeler
BOOKS COMING SOON!

Find out what happens next in:
Gunner and Daisy Go to the Ranch